Anonymous

The Parlor Muse

A selection of Vers de Société from modern poets

Anonymous

The Parlor Muse
A selection of Vers de Société from modern poets

ISBN/EAN: 9783337278373

Printed in Europe, USA, Canada, Australia, Japan

Cover: Foto ©Andreas Hilbeck / pixelio.de

More available books at **www.hansebooks.com**

Anonymous

The Parlor Muse
A selection of Vers de Société from modern poets

ISBN/EAN: 9783337278373

Printed in Europe, USA, Canada, Australia, Japan

Cover: Foto ©Andreas Hilbeck / pixelio.de

More available books at **www.hansebooks.com**

𝔓𝔞𝔯𝔠𝔥𝔪𝔢𝔫𝔱-𝔓𝔞𝔭𝔢𝔯 𝔖𝔢𝔯𝔦𝔢𝔰.

The Parlor Muse:

A SELECTION OF

VERS DE SOCIÉTÉ

FROM MODERN POETS.

☙☙

NEW YORK:

D. Appleton & Co., 1, 3, & 5 Bond Street.

1884.

Contents.

Contents.

The Parlor Muse.

• ● •

THE BELLE OF THE BALL-ROOM.

YEARS—years ago—ere yet my dreams
    Had been of being wise or witty—
Ere I had done with writing themes,
    Or yawned o'er this infernal Chitty;—
Years—years ago—while all my joy
    Was in my fowling-piece and filly,—
In short, while I was yet a boy,
    I fell in love with Laura Lily.

I saw her at the County Ball:
    There, where the sounds of flute and fiddle

Gave signal sweet, in that old hall,
  Of hands across and down the middle,
Hers was the subtlest spell by far
  Of all that set young hearts romancing;
She was our queen, our rose, our star;
  And then she danced—O Heaven, her danc-
    ing!

Dark was her hair, her hand was white;
  Her voice was exquisitely tender;
Her eyes were full of liquid light;
  I never saw a waist so slender!
Her every look, her every smile,
  Shot right and left a score of arrows;
I thought 'twas Venus from her isle,
  And wondered where she'd left her sparrows.

She talked,—of politics or prayers,—
  Or Southey's prose, or Wordsworth's son-
    nets,—
Of danglers—or of dancing bears,
  Of battles—or the last new bonnets;

By candlelight, at twelve o'clock,
   To me it mattered not a tittle ;
If those bright lips had quoted Locke,
   I might have thought they murmured Little.

Through sunny May, through sultry June,
   I loved her with a love eternal;
I spoke her praises to the moon,
   I wrote them to the " Sunday Journal."
My mother laughed ; I soon found out
   That ancient ladies have no feeling;
My father frowned ; but how should gout
   See any happiness in kneeling ?

She was the daughter of a Dean—
   Rich, fat, and rather apoplectic ;
She had one brother, just thirteen,
   Whose color was extremely hectic ;
Her grandmother for many a year
   Had fed the parish with her bounty ;
Her second cousin was a peer,
   And Lord-Lieutenant of the county.

But titles, and the three per cents,
  And mortgages, and great relations,
And India bonds, and tithes, and rents—
  Oh! what are they to love's sensations?
Black eyes, fair forehead, clustering locks—
  Such wealth, such honors Cupid chooses;
He cares as little for the Stocks
  As Baron Rothschild for the Muses.

She sketched; the vale, the wood, the beach,
  Grew lovelier from her pencil's shading.
She botanized; I envied each
  Young blossom in her boudoir fading:
She warbled Handel; it was grand;
  She made the Catalini jealous:
She touched the organ; I could stand
  For hours and hours to blow the bellows.

She kept an album, too, at home,
  Well filled with all an album's glories:
Paintings of butterflies, and Rome,
  Patterns for trimmings, Persian stories;

Soft songs to Julia's cockatoo,
  Fierce odes to Famine and to Slaughter,
And autographs of Prince Leboo,
  And recipes for elder-water.

And she was flattered, worshiped, bored ;
  Her steps were watched, her dress was noted ;
Her poodle dog was quite adored,
  Her sayings were extremely quoted.
She laughed, and every heart was glad,
  As if the taxes were abolished ;
She frowned, and every look was sad,
  As if the Opera were demolished.

She smiled on many, just for fun—
  I knew that there was nothing in it ;
I was the first—the only one
  Her heart had thought of for a minute.—
I knew it, for she told me so,
  In phrase which was divinely molded ;
She wrote a charming hand—and oh !
  How sweetly all her notes were folded !

Our love was like most other loves—
    A little glow, a little shiver,
A rose-bud, and a pair of gloves,
    And " Fly not yet "—upon the river;
Some jealousy of some one's heir,
    Some hopes of dying broken-hearted,
A miniature, a lock of hair,
    The usual vows—and then we parted.

We parted; months and years rolled by;
    We met again four summers after.
Our parting was all sob and sigh,
    Our meeting was all mirth and laughter:
For in my heart's most secret cell
    There had been many other lodgers;
And she was not the ball-room's Belle,
    But only—Mrs. Something Rogers!

                        WINTHROP M. PRAED.

TU QUOQUE.

An Idyl in the Conservatory.

NELLIE.

IF I were you, when ladies at the play, sir,
  Beckon and nod, a melodrama through,
I would not turn abstractedly away, sir,
  If I were you!

FRANK.

If I were you, when persons I affected
  Wait for three hours to take me down to
    Kew,
I would, at least, pretend I recollected,
  If I were you!

NELLIE.

If I were you, when ladies are so lavish,
  Sir, as to keep me every waltz but two,
I would not dance with *odious* Miss M'Tavish,
  If I were you!

FRANK.

If I were you, who vow you can not suffer
  Whiff of the best,—the mildest "honey-dew,"
I would not dance with smoke-consuming
    Puffer,
  If I were you!

NELLIE.

If I were you, I would not, sir, be bitter,
  Even to write the "Cynical Review;"—

FRANK.

No, I should doubtless find flirtation fitter,
  If I were you!

NELLIE.

Really! you would? Why, Frank, you're
    quite delightful—
  Hot as Othello, and as black of hue;
Borrow my fan. I would not look so *frightful,*
  If I were you!

FRANK.

" It is the cause "—I mean your chaperon is
  Bringing some well-curled juvenile. Adieu !
I shall retire. I'd spare that poor Adonis,
  If I were you !

NELLIE.

Go, if you will. At once ! and by express, sir !
  Where shall it be ? To China—or Peru ?
Go. I should leave inquirers my address, sir,
  If I were you !

FRANK.

No—I remain. To stay and fight a duel
  Seems, on the whole, the proper thing to do—
Ah, you are strong—I would not then be cruel,
  If I were you !

NELLIE.

One does not like one's feelings to be doubted,—

FRANK.

One does not like one's friends to misconstrue,—

NELLIE.

If I confess that I a wee-bit pouted?—

FRANK.

I should admit that I was *piqué*, too.

NELLIE.

Ask me to dance.   I'd say no more about it,
    If I were you !   (Waltz.—*Exeunt.*)

AUSTIN DOBSON.

INCOGNITA.

JUST for a space that I met her—
    Just for a day in the train !
It began when she feared it would wet her,
    That tiniest spurtle of rain :
So we tucked a great rug in the sashes,
    And carefully padded the pane ;
And I sorrow in sackcloth and ashes,
    Longing to do it again !

Then it grew when she begged me to reach her
    A dressing-case under the seat ;
She was " really so tiny a creature
    That she needed a stool for her feet ! "
Which was promptly arranged to her order
    With a care that was even minute,
And a glimpse—of an open-work border,
    And a glance—of the fairyest boot.

Then it drooped, and revived at some hovels—
    " Were they houses for men or for pigs ? "
Then it shifted to muscular novels,
    With a little digression on prigs :
She thought " Wives and Daughters " " *so*
        jolly ! "
    " Had I read it ? " She knew when I had,
Like the rest, I should dote upon " Molly ; "
    And " poor Mrs. Gaskell—how sad ! "

" Like Browning ? " " But so-so." His proof
        lay
    Too deep for her frivolous mood,

That preferred your mere metrical *soufflé*
    To the stronger poetical food;
Yet at times he was good—"as a tonic;"
    Was Tennyson writing just now?
And was this new poet Byronic,
    And clever, and naughty, or how?

Then we trifled with concerts and cro-
    quet,
    Then she daintily dusted her face;
Then she sprinkled herself with "Ess Bou-
    quet,"
    Fished out from the foregoing case;
And we chattered of Gassier and Grisi,
    And voted Aunt Sally a bore;
Discussed if the tight rope were easy,
    Or Chopin much harder than Spohr.

And oh! the odd things that she quoted,
    With the prettiest possible look,
And the price of two buns that she noted
    In the prettiest possible book,

While her talk like a musical rillet
  Flashed on with the hours that flew;
And the carriage, her smile seemed to fill it
  With just enough summer—for Two.

Till at last in her corner, peeping
  From a nest of rugs and of furs,
With the white shut eyelids sleeping
  On those dangerous looks of hers,
She seemed like a snowdrop breaking,
  Not wholly alive nor dead,
But with one blind impulse making
  To the sounds of the spring overhead;

And I watched in the lamplight's swerving
  The shade of the down-dropped lid,
And the lip-line's delicate curving,
  Where a slumbering smile lay hid,
Till I longed that, rather than sever,
  The train should shriek into space,
And carry us onward—forever—
  Me and that beautiful face.

2

But she suddenly woke in a fidget,
  With fears she was "nearly at home,"
And talked of a certain Aunt Bridget,
  Whom I mentally wished—well, at
    Rome;
Got out at the very next station,
  Looking back with a merry *Bon Soir*,
Adding, too, to my utter vexation,
  A surplus, unkind *Au Revoir*.

So left me to muse on her graces,
  To doze and to muse, till I dreamed
That we sailed through the sunniest places
  In a glorified galley, it seemed;
But the cabin was made of a carriage,
  And the ocean was Eau-de-Cologne,
And we split on a rock labeled MAR-
    RIAGE,
  And I woke—as cold as a stone.

And that's how I lost her—a jewel—
  Incognita—one in a crowd,

Not prudent enough to be cruel,
  Not worldly enough to be proud.
It was just a shut lid and its lashes,
  Just a few hours in a train,
And I sorrow in sackcloth and ashes,
  Longing to see her again !

AUSTIN DOBSON.

$$\rhd\!\circ\!\lhd$$

DORA *versus* ROSE.

" The case is proceeding."

FROM the tragic-est novels at Mudie's—
  At least, on a practical plan—
To the tales of mere Hodges and Judys,
  One love is enough for a man.
But no case that I ever yet met is
  Like mine: I am equally fond
Of Rose, who a charming brunette is,
        . And Dora, a blonde.

Each rivals the other in powers—
    Each waltzes, each warbles, each paints—
Miss Rose, chiefly tumble-down towers;
    Miss Do., perpendicular saints.
In short, to distinguish is folly;
    'Twixt the pair, I am come to the pass
Of Macheath between Lucy and Polly—
                Or Buridan's ass.

If it happens that Rose I have singled
    For a soft celebration in ryhme,
Then the ringlets of Dora get mingled
    Somehow with the tune and the time;
Or I painfully pen me a sonnet
    To an eyebrow intended for Do.'s,
And behold! I am writing upon it
                The legend, " To Rose."

Or I try to draw Dora (my blotter
    Is all overscrawled with her head);
If I fancy at last that I've got her,
    It turns to her rival instead;

Or I find myself placidly adding
　To the rapturous tresses of Rose
Miss Dora's bud-mouth, and her madding,
　　　　　　　Ineffable nose.

Was there ever so sad a dilemma?
　For Rose I would perish (*pro tem.*);
For Dora I'd willingly stem a—
　(Whatever might offer to stem);
But to make the invidious election—
　To declare that on either one's side
I've a scruple—a grain more affection,
　　　　　　　I *can not* decide.

And as either so hopelessly nice is,
　My sole and my final resource
Is to wait some indefinite crisis—
　Some feat of molecular force,
To solve me this riddle, conducive
　By no means to peace or repose,
Since the issue can scarce be inclusive
　　　　　　　Of Dora *and* Rose.

(After-thought.)

But, perhaps, if a third (say a Norah),
  Not quite so delightful as Rose—
Not wholy so charming as Dora—
  Should appear, is it wrong to suppose—
As the claims of the others are equal—
  And flight—in the main—is the best—
That I might . . . But no matter—the sequel
      Is easily guessed.

AUSTIN DOBSON.

▷◦◁

TO MY MISTRESS'S BOOTS.

THEY nearly strike me dumb,
And I tremble when they come
      Pit-a-pat:
This palpitation means
That these boots are Geraldine's,—
      Think of that.

O, where did hunter win
So delicate a skin
    For her feet?
You lucky little kid,
You perished, so you did,
    For my sweet!

The fairy stitching gleams
On the sides, and in the seams,
    And it shows
The Pixies were the wags
Who tipped these funny tags
    And these toes.

What soles to charm an elf!
Had Crusoe, sick of self,
    Chanced to view
One printed near the tide,
O, how hard he would have tried
    For the two!

For Gerry's debonair,
And innocent and fair
   As a rose.
She's an angel in a frock,
With a fascinating cock
   To her nose.

Those simpletons who squeeze
Their extremities, to please
   Mandarins,
Would positively flinch
From venturing to pinch
   Geraldine's.

Cinderella's *lefts and rights*
To Geraldine's were frights,
   And I trow
The damsel, deftly shod,
Has dutifully trod
   Until now.

Come, Gerry, since it suits
Such a pretty puss-in-boots
                    These to don,
Set this dainty hand awhile
On my shoulder, dear, and I'll
                    Put them on.

FREDERICK LOCKER.

HERMIONÉ.

WHEREVER I wander, up and about,
This is the puzzle I can't make out—
Because I care little for books, no doubt:

I have a wife, and she is wise,
  Deep in philosophy, strong in Greek;
Spectacles shadow her pretty eyes,
  Coteries rustle to hear her speak;
She writes a little—for love, not fame;

Has published a book with a dreary name;
   And yet (God bless her!) is mild and meek.
And how I happened to woo and wed
   A wife so pretty and wise withal,
Is part of the puzzle that fills my head—
Plagues me at day-time, racks me in bed,
   Haunts me, and makes me appear so small.
The only answer that I can see
Is—I could not have married Hermioné
(That is her fine wise name), but she
Stooped in her wisdom and married me.

For I am a fellow of no degree,
Given to romping and jollity;
The Latin they thrashed into me at school
   The world and its fights have thrashed
      away;
At figures alone I am no fool,
   And in city circles I say my say.
But I am a dunce at twenty-nine,
And the kind of study that I think fine

Is a chapter of Dickens, a sheet of the
    "Times"
  When I lounge, after work, in my easy-chair;
"Punch" for humor, and Praed for rhymes,
  And the butterfly *mots* blown here and there
  By the idle breath of the social air.
A little French is my only gift,
Wherewith at times I can make a shift,
Guessing at meanings, to flutter over
A filigree tale in a paper cover.

Hermioné, my Hermioné!
What could your wisdom perceive in me?
And, Hermioné, my Hermioné!
How does it happen at all that we
Love one another so utterly?
Well, I have a bright-eyed boy of two,
  A darling, who cries with lung and tongue
    about:
As fine a fellow, I swear to you,
  As ever poet of sentiment sung about!

And my lady-wife with the serious eyes
  Brightens and lightens when he is nigh,
And looks, although she is deep and wise,
  As foolish and happy as he or I !
And I have the courage just then, you see,
To kiss the lips of Hermioné—
Those learnèd lips that the learnèd praise—
And to clasp her close as in sillier days ;
To talk and joke in a frolic vein ;
  To tell her my stories of things and men ;
And it never strikes me that I am profane,
  For she laughs and blushes, and kisses
    again !
And presto ! fly goes her wisdom then !
The boy claps hands, and is up on her breast,
  Roaring to see her so bright with mirth ;
And I know she deems me (oh the jest !)
  The cleverest fellow on all the earth !

And Hermioné, my Hermioné,
Nurses her boy and defers to me ;

Does not seem to see I'm small—
Even to think me a dunce at all!
And wherever I wander, up and about,
Here is the puzzle I can't make out:
That Hermioné, my Hermioné,
In spite of her Greek and philosophy,
When sporting at night with her boy and
    me,
Seems sweeter and wiser, I assever—
Sweeter and wiser, and far more clever,
And makes me feel more foolish than ever,
Through her childish, girlish, joyous grace,
And the silly pride in her learnèd face!

That is the puzzle I can't make out—
Because I care little for books, no doubt;
But the puzzle is pleasant, I know not why,
  For, whenever I think of it, night or morn,
I thank my God she is wise, and I
  The happiest fool that was ever born.

ROBERT BUCHANAN.

"BEAUTY CLARE."

HALF Lucrece, half Messalina,
Lovely piece of Sèvres china,
　　When I see you, I compare
You with common, quiet creatures,
Homely delf in ways and features—
　　　　　Beauty Clare!

Surely Nature must have meant you
For a Siren when she sent you
　　That sweet voice and glittering hair;
Was it touch of human passion
Made you woman, in a fashion—
　　　　　Beauty Clare?

·I think not. The moral door-step
Cautiously you never o'erstep
　　When your victims you ensnare—

Lead them on with hopes—deceive them—
Then turn coldly round, and leave them,
            Beauty Clare.

Some new slave I note each season,
Wearing life away, his knees on
    (Moths around the taper's flare!)
Guardsman fine—or young attaché,
Black and smooth as papier-maché,
            Beauty Clare.

In your box I see them dangling,
Triumphs of successful angling,
    Trophies ranged behind your chair;
How they watch the fan you flutter!
How they drink each word you utter,
            Beauty Clare!

When at kettle-drums presiding,
I admire your tact, dividing
    Smiles to each, in equal share,

Lest one slave wax over-jealous,
Or another grow less zealous,
                Beauty Clare!

What perfection in your waltzing!
How in vain the women all sing
   When you warble some sweet air!
But your sentimental ditty
Over—you are then the witty
                Beauty Clare.

How you light the smoldering embers
Of decrepit Peers and Members!
   While you still have smiles to spare
For a new-fledged boy from college,
Sitting at *your* feet for knowledge!
                Beauty Clare!

At your country-seat in Salop,
What contention for a gallop
   With you on your chestnut mare!

How the country misses hate you,
Seeing o'er a five-barred gate—you,
   Beauty Clare!

All-accomplished little creature!
Fatally endowed by nature—
 Were your inward soul laid bare,
What should we discover under
That seductive mask, I wonder,
   Beauty Clare?

HAMILTON AÏDÉ.

• ⊞ •

UNDER THE TREES.

" UNDER the trees!" who but agrees
That there is magic in words such as these?
Promptly one sees shake in the breeze
Stately lime avenues haunted of bees:
Where, looking far over buttercupped leas,
Lads and "fair shes" (that is Byron's, and
  he's

3

An authority) lie very much at their ease,
Taking their teas, or their duck and green peas,
Or, if they prefer it, their plain bread and
    cheese :
Not objecting at all, though its rather a squeeze,
And the glass is, I daresay, at eighty degrees.
Some get up glees, and are mad about Ries,
And Sainton, and Tambulik's thrilling high C's ;
Or, if painter, hold forth upon Hunt and Maclise,
And the breadth of that landscape of Lee's ;
Or, if learned, on nodes and the moon's apo-
    gees ;
Or, if serious, on something of A. K. H. B.'s,
Or the latest attempt to convert the Chaldees ;
Or, in short, about all things, from earthquakes
    to fleas.
Some sit in twos or (less frequently) threes,
With their innocent lamb's-wool or book on
    their knees,
And talk and enact any nonsense you please,
As they gaze into eyes that are blue as the seas,

And you hear an occasional "Harry, don't
tease,"
From the sweetest of lips in the softest of
keys,
And other remarks which to me are Chinese.
And fast the time flees, till a lady-like sneeze,
Or a portly papa's more elaborate wheeze,
Makes Miss Tabitha seize on her brown muf-
fetees
And announce as a fact that it's going to
freeze,
And that young people ought to attend to their
P's
And their Q's, and not court every form of
disease.
Then Tommy eats up the three last ratafias,
And pretty Louise wraps her *robe de cerise*
Round a bosom as tender as Widow Machree's,
And (in spite of the pleas of her lorn *vis à vis*)
Goes and wraps up her uncle—a patient of
Skey's,

Who is prone to catch chills, like all old Ben-
    galese :—
But at bedtime I trust he'll remember to
    grease
The bridge of his nose, and preserve his
    rupees
From the premature clutch of his fond lega-
    tees;
Or at least have no fees to pay any M. D.'s
For the cold his niece caught sitting under the
    trees.

C. S. CALVERLEY.

A, B, C.

A is an Angel of blushing eighteen;
B is the Ball where the Angel was seen;
C is her Chaperon, who cheated at cards;
D is the Deuxtemps, with Frank of the Guards;
E is her Eye, killing slowly but surely;
F is the Fan, whence it peeped so demurely;

G is the Glove of superlative kid ;
H is the Hand which it spitefully hid ;
I is the Ice, which the fair one demanded ;
J is the Juvenile, that dainty who handed ;
K is the Kerchief, a rare work of art ;
L is the Lace which composed the chief part ;
M is the old Maid who watched the chits dance ;
N is the Nose she turned up at each glance ;
O is the Olga (just then in its prime) ;
P is the Partner who wouldn't keep time ;
Q is a Quadrille, put instead of the Lancers ;
R the Remonstrances made by the dancers ;
S is the Supper, where all went in pairs ;
T is the Twaddle they talked on the stairs ;
U is the Uncle who " thought he'd be goin' " ;
V is the Voice which his niece replied " No " in ;
W is the Waiter, who sat up till eight ;
X is his Exit, not rigidly straight ;
Y is a yawning fit caused by the Ball ;
Z stands for Zero, or nothing at all.

C. S. CALVERLEY.

FLIGHT.

O MEMORY! that which I gave thee
　　To guard in thy garner yestreen—
Little deeming thou e'er couldst behave thee
　　Thus basely—hath gone from thee clean!
Gone, fled, as ere autumn is ended
　　The yellow leaves flee from the oak—
I have lost it forever, my splendid
　　　　　　Original joke.

What was it?　I know I was brushing
　　My hair when the notion occurred:
I know that I felt myself blushing
　　As I thought, "How supremely absurd!
How they'll hammer on floor and on table
　　As its drollery dawns on them—how
They will quote it"—I wish I were able
　　　　　　To quote it just now.

I had thought to lead up conversation
  To the subject—it's easily done—
Then let off, as an airy creation
  Of the moment, that masterly pun.
Let it off, with a flash like a rocket's;
  In the midst of a dazzled conclave,
While I sat, with my hands in my pockets,
      The only one grave.

I had fancied young Titterton's chuckles,
  And old Bottleby's hearty guffaws
As he drove at my ribs with his knuckles,
  His mode of expressing applause:
While Jean Bottleby—queenly Miss Janet—
  Drew her handkerchief hastily out,
In fits at my slyness—what can it
      Have all been about?

I know 'twas the happiest, quaintest
  Combination of pathos and fun:
But I've got no idea—the faintest—
  Of what was the actual pun.

I think it was somehow connected
  With something I'd recently read—
Or heard—or perhaps recollected
      On going to bed.

What *had* I been reading? The "Standard":
  "Double Bigamy"; "Speech of the mayor."
And later—eh? yes! I meandered
  Through some chapters of "Vanity Fair."
How it fuses the grave with the festive!
  Yet e'en there, there is nothing so fine—
So playfully, subtly suggestive—
      As that joke of mine.

Did it hinge upon "parting asunder"?
  No, I don't part my hair with my brush.
Was the point of it "hair"? Now I wonder!
  Stop a bit—I shall think of it—hush! ·
There's *hare*, a wild animal.—Stuff!
  It was something a deal more recondite:
Of that I am certain enough;
      And of nothing beyond it.

Hair—*locks!* There are probably many
  Good things to be said about those.
Give me time—that's the best guess of any—
  " Lock " has several meanings, one knows.
Iron locks—*iron-gray locks*—a " deadlock "
  That would set up an every-day wit:
Then of course there's the obvious " wedlock ";
      But that wasn't it.

No! mine was a joke for the ages:
  Full of intricate meaning and pith;
A feast for your scholars and sages—
  How it would have rejoiced Sydney Smith!
'Tis such thoughts that ennoble a mortal;
  And, singling him out from the herd,
Fling wide immortality's portal—
      But what was the word?

Ah me! 'tis a bootless endeavor.
  As the flight of a bird of the air
Is the flight of a joke—you will never
  See the same one again, you may swear.

'Twas my first-born, and oh! how I prized it!
My darling, my treasure, my own!
This brain and none other devised it—
And now it has flown.

C. S. CALVERLEY.

FERDINANDO AND ELVIRA.

From "Bab Ballads."

PART I.

AT a pleasant evening party I had taken down
to supper
One whom I will call Elvira, and we talked of
love and Tupper,

Mr. Tupper and the poets, very lightly with
them dealing,
For I've always been distinguished for a strong
poetic feeling.

Then we let off paper crackers, each of which
    contained a motto,
And she listened while I read them, till her
    mother told her not to.

Then she whispered, "To the ball-room we
    had better, dear, be walking ;
If we stop down here much longer, really peo-
    ple will be talking."

There were noblemen in coronets, and military
    cousins,
There were captains by the hundred, there
    were baronets by dozens,

Yet she heeded not their offers, but dismissed
    them with a blessing ;
Then she let down all her back-hair which had
    taken long in dressing ;

Then she had convulsive sobbings in her agi-
    tated throttle,
Then she wiped her pretty eyes and smelt her
    pretty smelling-bottle.

So I whispered, "Dear Elvira, say—what can
the matter be with you?
Does anything you've eaten, darling Popsy,
disagree with you?"

But spite of all I said, her sobs grew more and
more distressing,
And she tore her pretty back-hair, which had
taken long in dressing.

Then she gazed upon the carpet, at the ceiling
then above me,
And she whispered, "Ferdinando, do you
really, *really* love me?"

"Love you?" said I, then I sighed, and then I
gazed upon her sweetly—
For I think I do this sort of thing particularly
neatly—

"Send me to the Arctic regions, or illimitable
azure,
On a scientific goose-chase, with my Coxwell
or my Glaisher!

"Tell me whither I may hie me, tell me, dear
    one, that I may know—
Is it up the highest Andes? down a horrible
    volcano?"

But she said, "It isn't polar bears, or hot vol-
    canic grottoes,
Only find out who it is that writes those lovely
    cracker mottoes!"

PART II.

"Tell me, Henry Wadsworth, Alfred, Poet
    Close, or Mister Tupper,
Do you write the bonbon mottoes my Elvira
    pulls at supper?"

But Henry Wadsworth smiled, and said he
    had not had that honor:
And Alfred, too, disclaimed the words that
    told so much upon her.

" Mister Martin Tupper, Poet Close, I beg of
you inform us ";
But my question seemed to throw them both
into a rage enormous.

Mister Close expressed a wish that he could
only get anigh to me.
And Mister Martin Tupper sent the following
reply to me:

" A fool is bent upon a twig, but wise men
dread a bandit,"
Which I know was very clever; but I didn't
understand it.

Seven weary years I wandered—Patagonia,
China, Norway,
Till at last I sank exhausted at a pastry-cook
his doorway.

There were fuchsias and geraniums, and daffo-
dils and myrtle,
So I entered, and I ordered half a basin of
mock turtle.

He was plump and he was chubby, he was
    smooth and he was rosy,
And his little wife was pretty, and particularly
    cozy.

And he chirped and sang, and skipped about,
    and laughed with laughter hearty—
He was wonderfully active for so very stout a
    party.

And I said, "O gentle pieman, why so very,
    very merry?
Is it purity of conscience, or your one-and-
    seven sherry?"

But he answered, "I'm so happy—no profes-
    sion could be dearer—
If I am not humming 'Tra! la! la!' I'm sing-
    ing 'Tirer, lirer!'

"First I go and make the patties, and the pud-
    dings and the jellies,
Then I make a sugar bird-cage, which upon a
    table swell is;

"Then I polish all the silver, which a supper-
　　table lacquers;
Then I write the pretty mottoes which you
　　find inside the crackers—"

"Found at last!" I madly shouted. "Gentle
　　pieman, you astound me!"
Then I waved the turtle-soup enthusiastically
　　round me!

And I shouted and I danced until he'd quite a
　　crowd around him—
And I rushed away, exclaiming, "I have found
　　him! I have found him!"

And I heard the gentle pieman in the road be-
　　hind me trilling,
"'Tira! lira!' stop him, stop him! 'Tra! la!
　　la!' the soup's a shilling!"

But until I reached Elvira's home, I never,
　　never waited,
And Elvira to her Ferdinand's irrevocably
　　mated!　　　　　WILLIAM S. GILBERT.

UP THE AISLE—NELL LATIM'S WEDDING.

TAKE my cloak—and now fix my veil, Jenny;
　　How silly to cover one's face!
I might as well be an old woman;
　　But then there's one comfort—it's lace.
Well, what *has* become of those ushers!
　　O pa! have you got my bouquet?—
I'll freeze standing here in the lobby—
　　Why doesn't the organist play?—
They're started at last—what a bustle!—
　　Stop, pa!—they're not far enough—wait!
One minute more—now!—*do* keep step, pa!
　　There, drop my trail, Jane!—is it straight?
I hope I look timid, and shrinking;
　　The church must be perfectly full—
Good gracious! now *don't* walk so fast, pa!—
　　He don't seem to think that trains pull.
The chancel at last—mind the step, pa!—
　　I don't feel embarrassed at all.—

4

But, my! what's the minister saying?
　　Oh, I know; that part 'bout Saint Paul.
I hope my position is graceful;
　　How awkwardly Nelly Dane stood!—
" Not lawfully be joined together—
　　Now speak "—as if any one would!—
Oh, dear! now it's my turn to answer—
　　I do wish that pa would stand still.
" Serve him, love, honor, and keep him "—
　　How sweetly he says it!—I will.
Where's pa?—there, I knew he'd forget it,
　　When the time came to give me away—
" I, Helena, take thee—love—cherish—
　　And "—well, I can't help it—" obey."
Here, Maud, take my bouquet—don't drop
　　　it!
　　I hope Charley's not lost the ring;
Just like him!—no!—goodness, how heavy!
　　It's really an elegant thing.
It's a shame to kneel down in white satin—
　　And the flounce, real old lace—but I
　　　must;

I hope they've got a clean cushion,
  They're usually covered with dust.
All over—ah! thanks!—now, don't fuss, pa!—
  Just throw back my veil, Charley—there—
Oh, bother! why couldn't he kiss me
  Without mussing up all my hair!—
Your arm, Charley, there goes the organ—
  Who'd think there would be such a
    crowd?
Oh, I mustn't look round, I'd forgotten—
  See, Charley, who was it that bowed?
Why—it's Nelly Allaire with her husband—
  She's awfully jealous, I know;
'Most all of my things were imported,
  And she had a home-made trousseau,
And there's Annie Wheeler — Kate Her-
    mon,—
  I didn't expect her at all,—
If she's not in that same old blue satin
  She wore at the Charity Ball!
Is that Fanny Wade?—Edith Pearton—
  And Emma, and Jo—all the girls?

I knew they'd not miss my wedding—
  I hope they'll all notice my pearls.
Is the carriage there?—give me my cloak,
    Jane—
  Don't get it all over my veil—
No! you take the other seat, Charley,
  I need all this for my trail.

                  GEORGE A. BAKER, JR.

TO YOUNGSTERS.

GOLDEN hair and eyes of blue,—
What won't they do?—what won't they do?
Eyes of blue and locks of gold—
My boy, you'll learn before you're old.
The gaitered foot, the taper waist—
Be not in haste, be not in haste;
Before your chin sprout twenty spear,
My word for 't, youngster, they'll appear.

Raven hair and eyes of night
Undo the boys (it serves 'em right);
Eyes of night and raven hair,
They'll drive you, Hopeful, to despair.
The drooping curl, the downward glance,
They're only waiting for the chance;
At nick of time they'll sure appear,
Depend upon it, laddie dear.

Shapely hands and arms of snow,
They know their charm, my boy, they know;
Flexile wrists and fleckless hands,
The lass that has them understands.
The cheeks that blush, the lips that smile—
A little while, a little while—
Before you know it, they'll be here,
And catch you napping, laddie dear.

Hands, and hair, and lips, and eyes—
'Tis there the tyro's danger lies.
You'll meet them leagued, or one by one;
In either case the mischief's done.

A touch, a tress, a glance, a sigh,
And then, my boy, good-by—good-by!
God help you, youngster! keep good cheer;
Coax on your chin to twenty spear.

JOHN VANCE CHENEY.

From "The Century Magazine."

THE HAT.

Recited by M. Coquelin, of the Comédie Française.

[In Paris, monologues are the fashion. Some are in verse; some are in prose. At every matinée, dinner-party, or *soirée* the mistress of the entertainment makes it her duty to provide some little scenic recitation, to be gone through by Saint-Germain or Coquelin. One which recently enjoyed great success entitled "The Hat," we here offer in an English version.]

Mise en Scène: A gentleman holding his hat.

WELL, yes! On Tuesday last the knot was
    tied—
Tied hard and fast; that can not be denied.

The Hat.

I'm caught, I'm caged, from the law's point of
    view,
Before two witnesses, good men and true.
I'm licensed, stamped: undo the deed who can;
Three hundred francs made me a married
    man.

  Who would have thought it! Married!
    How? What for?
I who was ranked a strict old bachelor;
I who through halls with married people
    crammed
Infused a kind of odor of the damned;
I who declined—and gave lame reasons why—
Five, six, good comfortable matches; I
Who every morning when I came to dress
Found I had one day more, and some hairs
    less;
I whom all mothers slander and despise,
Because girls find no favor in my eyes—
Married! A married man! Beyond—a—
    doubt!

How, do you ask, came such a thing about?
What prompted *me* to dare connubial bliss?
What worked the wondrous metamorphosis?
What made so great a change—a change like
    that?
Imagine. Guess. You give it up?
                      A hat!

A hat, in short, like all the hats you see—
A plain silk stove-pipe hat. *This* did for me.
A plain black hat, just like the one that's here.

  A hat?
      Why, yes.
            But how?
                  Well, lend an ear.

One day this winter I went out to dine.
All was first-rate—the style, the food, the wine.
A concert afterward—*en règle*—just so.
The hour arrived. I entered, bowing low,
My heels together. Then I placed my hat
On something near, and joined the general chat.

At half-past eight we dined.   All went off well.
Trust me for being competent to tell!
I sat between two ladies—mute as fishes—
With nothing else to do but count the dishes.
I learned each item in each course by heart.
I hate tobacco, but as smoke might part
Me from those ladies, with a sober face
I took a strong cigar, and kept my place.
The concert was announced for half-past ten,
And at that hour I joined a crowd of men.
The ladies, arm to arm, sweet, white, we
        found,
Like rows of sugared almonds, seated round.
I leaned against the door—there was no chair.
A stout, fierce gentleman, got up with care
(A cuirassier I set him down to be),
Leaned on the other door-post, hard by me,
Whilst far off in the distance some poor girl
Sang, with her love-lorn ringlets out of curl,
Some trashy stuff of love and love's distress.
I could see nothing, and could hear still less.
Still, I applauded, for politeness' sake.

Next a dress-coat of fashionable make
Came forward and began. It clad a poet.
That's the last mode in Paris. Did you know it?
Your host or hostess, after dinner, chooses
To serve you up some effort of the Muses,
Recited with *vim*, gestures, and by-play
By some one borrowed from the great Fran-
    çaise.

    I blush to write it—poems, you must know,
All make me sleepy ; and it was so now.
For as I listened to the distant drone
Of the smooth lines, I felt my lids droop down,
And a strange torpor I could not ignore
Came creeping o'er me.
                " Heavens! suppose I snore !
Let me get out," I cried, " or else—"
                                With that
I cast my eyes around to find my hat.

    The *console* where I laid it down, alas!
Was now surrounded (not a mouse could pass)

By triple rows of ladies gayly dressed,
Who fanned and listened calmly, undistressed.
No man through that fair crowd could work
     his way.
Rank behind rank rose heads in bright array.
Diamonds were there, and flowers, and, lower
     still,
Such lovely shoulders! Not the smallest thrill
They raised in me. My thoughts were of my
     hat.
It lay beyond where all those ladies sat,
Under a candelabrum, shiny, bright,
Smooth as when last I brushed it, full in sight,
Whilst I, far off, with yearning glances tried
Whether I could not lure it to my side.

" Why may my hand not put thee on my head,
And quit this stifling room?" I fondly said.
" Respond, dear hat, to a magnetic throb.
Come, little darling; cleave this female mob.
Fly over heads; creep under. Come, oh, come!
Escape. We'll find no poetry at home."

And all the while did that dull poem creep
Drearily on, till, sick at last with sleep,
My eyes fixed straight before me with a stare,
I groaned within me:
                    "Come, my hat—fresh air!
My darling, let us both get out together.
Here all is hot and close; outside, the weather
Is simply perfect, and the pavement's dry.
Come, come, my hat—one effort! Do but try.
Sweet thoughts the silence and soft moon will stir
Beneath thy shelter."
                    Here a voice cried:
                                        "Sir,
Have you done staring at my daughter yet?
By Jove! sir."
                    My astonished glance here met
The angry red face of my cuirassier.
I did not quail before his look severe,
But said, politely,
                    "Pardon, sir, but I
Do not so much as know her."
                                "What, sir! Why,

My daughter's yonder, sir, beside that table.
Pink ribbons, sir. Don't tell me you're un-
able
To understand."
          " But, sir—"
                    " I don't suppose
You mean to tell me—"
            " Really—"
                " Who but knows
Your way of dealing with young ladies,
sir?
I'll have no trifling, if you please, with her."
" Trifling?"
        " Yes, sir. You know you've jilted five.
Every one knows it—every man alive."
" Allow me—"
           " No, sir. Every father knows
Your reputation, damaging to those
Who—"
      " Sir, indeed—"
            " How dare you in this place
Stare half an hour in my daughter's face?"

"*Sapristi, monsieur!* I protest—I swear—
I never looked at her."

      "Indeed! What were
You looking at, then?"

       "Sir, I'll tell you *that*—
My hat, sir."

     "*Morbleu!* looking at your hat!"
"Yes, sir, it *was* my hat."

       My color rose:
He angered me, this man who would suppose
I thought of nothing but his girl.

        Meantime
The black coat maundered on in dreary rhyme.
Papa and I, getting more angry ever,
Exchanged fierce glances, speaking both to-
   gether,
While no one round us knew what we were at.
"It was my daughter, sir."

      "No, sir—my hat."
"Speak lower, gentlemen," said some one near.
"You'll give account for this, sir. Do you
   hear?"

" Of course, sir."

        " Then before the world's astir,
You'll get my card, sir."

          " I'll be ready, sir."

A pretty quarrel! Don't you think it so?
A moment after, all exclaimed, " Bravo!"
Black coat had finished. All the audience
     made
A general move toward ice and lemonade.
The coast was clear; my way was open
     now;
My hat was mine. I made my foe a bow,
And hastened, fast as lover could have moved,
Through trailing trains, toward the dear thing
     I loved.
I tried to reach it.

        " Here's the hat, I think,
You are in search of."

        Shapely, soft, and pink,
A lovely arm, a perfect arm, held out
My precious hat. Impelled by sudden doubt,

I raised my eyes. Pink ribbons trimmed her
    dress.
" Here, monsieur, take it. 'Twas not hard to
    guess
What made you look this way. You longed
    to go.
You were so sleepy, nodding—see !—just so.
Ah, how I wished to help you, if I could !
I might have passed it possibly. I would
Have tried by ladies' chain, from hand to hand,
To send it to you, but, you understand,
I felt a little timid—don't you see ?—
For fear they might suppose—Ah ! pardon me ;
I am too prone to talk. I'm keeping you.
Take it. Good-night."
                Sweet angel, pure and true !
My looks to their real cause *she* could refer,
And never thought one glance was meant for
    her.

Oh, simple trust, pure from debasing wiles !
I took my hat from her fair hand with smiles,

And hurrying back, sought out my whilom foe,
Exclaiming:

        "Hear me, sir. Before I go,
Let me explain. You, sir, were in the right.
'Twas not my hat attracted me to-night.
Forgive me, pardon me, I entreat, dear sir.
I love your daughter, and I gazed at her."
"You, sir?"

        He turned his big round eyes on me,
Then held his hand out.

          "Well, well, we will see."

   Next day we talked. That's how it came
     about.
And the result you see. My secret's out.
It was last Tuesday, as I said, and even
Add, she's an angel, and my home is—heaven.
Her father, mild in spite of mien severe,
Holds a high office—is no cuirassier.
Besides—a boon few bridegrooms can com-
     mand—
He is a widower—so—you understand.

   5

Now all this happiness, beyond a doubt,
By this silk hat I hold was brought about,
Or by its brother. Poor old English tile!
Many have sneered at thy ungainly style;
Many, with ridicule and gibe—why not?—
Have dubbed thee "stove-pipe," called thee
       "chimney-pot."
They, as æsthetes, are not far wrong, maybe;
But I, for all that thou hast done for me,
Raise thee, in spite of nonsense sung or said,
With deep respect, and place thee on my head.

From Harper's Magazine, by permission.   Translation of
MRS. E. W. LATIMER.

JUST A LOVE–LETTER.

NEW YORK, *July* 20, 1883.

DEAR GIRL:
        The town goes on as though
It thought you still were in it;

The gilded cage seems scarce to know
　That it has lost its linnet.
The people come, the people pass;
　The clock keeps on a-ticking;
And through the basement plots of grass
　Persistent weeds are pricking.

I thought 'twould never come—the Spring—
　Since you had left the city;
But on the snow-drifts lingering
　At last the skies took pity.
Then Summer's yellow warmed the sun,
　Daily decreasing distance—
I really don't know how 'twas done
　Without your kind assistance.

Aunt Van, of course, still holds the fort:
　I've paid the call of duty;
She gave me one small glass of port—
　'Twas '34 and fruity.
The furniture was draped in gloom
　Of linen brown and wrinkled;

I smelt in spots about the room
  The pungent camphor sprinkled.

I sat upon the sofa where
  You sat and dropped your thimble—
You know—you said you didn't care;
  But I was nobly nimble.
On hands and knees I dropped, and tried
  To—well, I tried to miss it:
You slipped your hand down by your side—
  You knew I meant to kiss it!

Aunt Van, I fear we put to shame
  Propriety and precision;
But, praised be Love, that kiss just came
  Beyond your line of vision.
Dear maiden aunt! the kiss, more sweet
  Because 'tis surreptitious,
You never stretched a hand to meet,
  So dimpled, dear, delicious.

I sought the Park last Saturday;
  I found the Drive deserted;

The water-trough beside the way
  Sad and superfluous spurted.
I stood where Humboldt guards the gate,
  Bronze, bumptious, stained, and streaky—
There sat a sparrow on his pate,
  A sparrow chirp and cheeky.

Ten months ago! Ten months ago!—
  It seems a happy second,
Against a lifetime lone and slow,
  By Love's wild time-piece reckoned—
You smiled, by Aunt's protecting side,
  Where thick the drags were massing,
On one young man who didn't ride,
  But stood and watched you passing.

I haunt Purssell's—to his amaze—
  Not that I care to eat there,
But for the dear clandestine days
  When we two had to meet there.
Oh, blessèd is that baker's bake,
  Past cavil and past question:

I ate a bun for your sweet sake,
  And memory helped digestion.

The Norths are at their Newport ranch;
  Van Brunt has gone to Venice;
Loomis invites me to the Branch,
  And lures me with lawn tennis.
O bustling barracks by the sea!
  O spiles, canals, and islands!
Your varied charms are naught to me—
  My heart is in the Highlands!

My paper trembles in the breeze
  That all too faintly flutters
Among the dusty city trees,
  And through my half-closed shutters:
A northern captive in the town,
  Its native vigor deadened,
I hope that, as it wandered down,
  Your dear pale cheek it reddened.

I'll write no more!   A *vis-à-vis*
  In halcyon vacation

Will sure afford a much more free
  Mode of communication.
I'm tantalized and cribbed and checked
  In making love by letter:
I know a style more brief, direct—
  And generally better!

By permission.   H. C. BUNNER.

"POSSUM"—I CAN.

HER eyes are as blue as the heart of a berg;
  If tears from their channels e'er ran,
If they melted an instant, it was not in ruth
  For sorrows of love or of man.

I've wondered ofttimes—she's so frostily fair—
  If blood in her veins really ran;
While sipping an ice I've asked myself where
  Ice ended and woman began.

"My heart," she once told me, "is dead as
          a stone,
   Or missing in Nature's nice plan;
Some women, perhaps, can not live without
          hearts,"
   Her eyes spoke a haughty "I can."

The stingiest sultan would lay at her feet
   The wealth of a whole Ispahan.
Independent in fortune as well as in soul,
   She scorns every suppliant man.

Her coach, of all turn-outs this year at the
          Springs,
   Was drawn by the handsomest span;
Her crest on its panels, a leopard *passant*,
   Her motto is " Possum "—I can.

Regarding the carriage with critical air
   Up-spoke our head-waiter, black Dan:
"Some folks, maybe, can't see no difference
          between
   Dat ting and a 'possum—I can.

" Why, dat ain't no 'possum ; it's more like a
    cat,
Or Spot, dar, your pert black-and-tan :
I ought to know 'possums—I'se hunted 'em
    till
Each 'possum in Georgia knows Dan.

" Curusest ob varmints dar is in dis world
    Is 'possums and women," said Dan ;
" Dey's nebber so sleek, so indif'rent, and
    cool,
As when dey's deceibing some man.

" I 'members de fust one dat ever I cotched—
    It tried de same little ole plan :
I found it like dead at the foot ob a tree ;
    Says I, ' No *dead* 'possums for Dan'—

" Was walking away when it opened one eye,
    Larfed back ob its paw, and den—ran !
' Can't come it,' it said, plain as eber you
    heard ;
Says I, ' Missus 'Possum, I can.' "

The tale was a short one, and not too refined,
  As told by our swart Caliban:
It fed, by the thought it aroused in my mind,
  The fire of my hopes like a fan.

Could *she* play at *'possum,* her heart all alive
  And craving the love of a man,
Worth love and worth trust, can I credit the
    thought?
  My heart made me answer—"I can."

Her soul *is* alive, and now tell me, my heart,
  Canst rise to the fate like a man,
Receiving thy doom or thy bliss from her
    lips?
  Again I heard, "Possum—I can."

"You can love?"   The answer is easily
    guessed
  (Fit rallying-cry for a clan),
It came with a kiss, and a ring with the crest
  A leopard: 'twas "Possum—I can!"

LIZZIE W. CHAMPNEY.

PAST AND PRESENT; OR, ROMANCE *VERSUS* REALITY.

A Duet.

HE (*shutting his Froissart with a slap*).

" OH, for the days of olden time,
　When, true to knightly duty,
The champion roved through every clime
　To win the smile of Beauty!
'Neath moonlit skies his midnight spent,
　In place of ball-rooms choky,
And through triumphal arches went,
　Instead of hoops at croquet!"

SHE (*smiling maliciously*).

" Ha, ha! nice figure *you'd* have made
　'Mid Syria's heat and slaughter,
Who growl at seventy in the shade,
　And long for seltzer-water!

I think I hear you mutter, then,
    While through the sand-heaps wading:
' Well, let me once get home again,
    And deuce take all crusading ! ' "

HE.

" You heartless thing ! but *you* have ne'er
    Perused, like me, their story—
Who knew no task they would not dare,
    No pain when crowned with glory;
And, glowing o'er those pages dear,
    I've wished, with heart o'erladen,
I were a Spanish cavalier
    And you my chosen maiden ! "

SHE.

" O Fred, you goose ! I ne'er could bide
    Unseen behind a grating,
Nor bear forever at my side
    A prim duenna waiting.

And then this face you *say* you prize,
  Some horrid Moor might eye it,
And whisk me off before your eyes—"

HE (*fiercely*).

"I'd like to see him try it!"

SHE.

"Then, too, in that stern age, you know,
  No opera, ball, nor fashion,
No lovely sleighing in the snow,
  No novels filled with passion.
In convent lone, or castle strong,
  It *must* have been diverting
To stitch at tap'stry all day long,
  With ne'er a chance of flirting!"

HE.

"Of course, that's the thing you require!
  But men had then a chance, dear,
To win their spurs through gore and mire
  In Palestine or France, dear:

And when the stubborn fray was done,
  His lady crowned the winner,
And—"

SHE.

" Pawned the spurs his strife had won,
  To buy their Sunday dinner!"

HE (*angrily*),

" Too bad, by Jove! of all I say
  You will make fun—"

SHE.

                    " Poor fellow!
He sees *en beau* our fathers' day,
  But ours in jaundiced yellow.
Your knights, good sir (whose spurs of gold
  Were all the wealth they carried),
Oft found their 'chosen maidens' cold,
  And lived (or died) unmarried!

"But never mind, dear Fred; for, though
  I sometimes like to tease you,

I'd never say a word, you know,
　　That really could displease you;
And, though papa may fume and rage,
　　And vow he'll ne'er endure it,
Just wait until I come of age,
　　And then—"

HE (*ecstatically*).

"The ring and curate!"

DAVID KER.

●—●—●

FREE, OR CAGED.

A Cousinly Duet.

FLORA (*with significant emphasis*).

SEE, birdie! here's your seed and cake,
　　And here's your water handy;
Come, trim your yellow plumes and make
　　Your little self a dandy!

You're wiser far than *some* I know,
　Who, home and comfort scorning,
Through every sort of danger go,
　And won't take friendly warning.

FRANK (*defiantly*).

So be it.　"Home and comfort" I
　Can leave to those who need 'em;
Mine the wide earth, the open sky,
　The wanderer's life of freedom!
And—

FLORA.

Better far at home to stay
　Than burn abroad or shiver;
There's nothing there can match our bay,
　Or beat our Hudson River!

FRANK (*wth profound irony*).

Forth, then, O Frank! in vent'rous bark
Round Coney Island sailing,

Exploring wilds of Central Park,
　　Or Brooklyn bridge-tower scaling!
Ho, bring my boots! I burn to gain
　　Famed Harlem's mountains broken,
And flaunt in Scribner's window-pane
　　My " Travels through Hoboken!"

FLORA.

You wretch! how dare you mock me so
　　At every word I utter?

FRANK (*proudly*).

Well, I'm no cage-bred pet, you know,
　　To chirp for cake-and-butter;
Mine be the wild-bird's rocky lair,
　　The wild-bird's flight aspiring,
To soar through boundless realms of air
　　On pinions never tiring!

FLORA (*sarcastically*).

But when the cold December blast
　　Through leafless boughs came moaning,

6

Or stones by impish urchins cast
  Your carols turned to groaning,
I guess you'd find your " freedom " sweet
  Too cold for admiration,
And change for birdie's cage and meat
  Your free, unthralled starvation.

FRANK.

Bah ! give to those who fear the strife,
  Retirement and a cottage ;
No Esau I to barter life
  And all it yields for pottage !
Not all the gold of Wall Street Jews
  To one dull spot should pin me,
With " earth before me where to choose,"
  And life aglow within me !

FLORA.

Ah me ! no cloud the spirit dims
  Till youth and vigor fail us ;
But when gray hairs and feeble limbs
  And creeping years assail us,

When now no more we proudly stand
  Defying grief and dangers,
'Tis then we miss the loving hand—
  Lone in a world of strangers!

FRANK (*smiling*).

Aha! there spoke the sex, *ma mie!*
  No song but this one only:
" Get married and thrice happy be—
  Live single and be lonely!"
Well, well, don't frown, my pretty sage—
  You know my tongue's a railer;
But, if I'm destined to the cage,
  Will *you*, dear, be my jailer?

DAVID KER.

—●—○—●—

IN THE CONSERVATORY.

" BUT we *must* return! What *will* they say?
  Yes, I know it's awful nice
In the window here, from the others away,
  With a taste, now and then, of the ice,

And now and then of— Oh, you wretch!
  It wasn't at all required
That you should illustrate thus with a sketch
  The speech that of course you admired.

" No matter how naughty. There! you have
     spoiled
  The ' classical Grecian knot '
In which you like my hair to be coiled,
  And I really don't know what
Other mischief you haven't done! You're
     just
  Real naughty! You squeeze like a vise!
Why can't you men take something on
     trust,
  And be more dainty and nice?

" There! I'm ready, now. What! *just one*
     more ?
  Oh! aren't you a darling tease?
And love me so?—*one, two, three, four !*
  There! come now, dearest, please!

I'm almost afraid of the parlor glare :
 When they look at my lips, they'll see
The kisses upon them."—"*No, not there ;*
 But, sweet, in your eyes maybe."

EARL MARBLE.

THE AMATEUR SPELLING–MATCH.

SINCE spelling-matches everywhere
 O'er all the land abound,
Why should not we, too, "do and dare?"
 I will the words propound,
And you the "favored scholar" be,
 As Rogers' group suggests.
With what a wealth of poetry
 The subject he invests !

Spell "spoons." "What! such a word!"
  you say?
 "But fit for kitchen-school?

Or, in New Orleans, far away,
  When under Butler's rule?"
Fie! fie! should social science come,
  Or scurvy politics,
To mar our peace with brutal bomb?
  Away with all such tricks!

There! please go on. "S"—oh! the sound
  Through lips that sweetly smile,
Like sibilant waters unprofound,
  That aimless hours beguile
On pebbly beaches! "P"—more staid
  The smile now on the lips,
As though love's sun that warmed the
      maid
  Was partly 'neath eclipse.

"Double o"—through parting lips that
      breaks,
  Like gurgling rill half held
'Tween walling rocks and tent-like brakes,
  And wonder semi-knelled

Through circling lips. " N "—here again
   The semi-smile that played
Athwart your lips so sweetly when
   The " s " you first essayed.

"S"—ah! the smile is here again !
   Oh, sweet thou letter "s"!
You 'mind me of that moment when
   A tremulous little " Yes "
From self-same lips a day in eld
   My being thrilled with joy—
When clouds of doubt were quick dispelled,
   And life lost all alloy.

" Quite right," I said ; " but why this waste
   Of letters, since with two
It can be spelled with greater haste,
   More truth, and less ado?
" Oh, fie ! S, p, double o, n, s,
   Spells ' spoons ' : you needn't try
To spell the word with any less."
   " Yes, dear ; two—'*u* and *I.*' "

                              EARL MARBLE.

A CHURCH-GOING BELLE.

A DAINTY little bonnet,
　　The sweetest marabout,
A sea of tawny wavelets
　　O'er forehead white as snow;
A brace of sparkling sapphires,
　　Two cheeks of rosy dye,
A pair of lips of ruby,
　　And a fascinating sigh.
Think'st thou she goes to worship?
　　Ah! it is difficult to tell,
But it's plain both saints and sinners
　　Worship that Sabbath belle.

A tightly-fitting bodice,
　　Costume all brocaded,
Short petticoats with flounces,
　　In endless colors braided;
Enameled shoes with buckles,
　　Such as the Frenchmen vend,

With lofty, taper heel-taps,
   To give a Grecian bend.
Think'st thou it 's for God's glory
   She dresses out so well?
Or does she want some saint or sinner
   To love the Sabbath belle?

ANONYMOUS.

I WISH HE WOULD DECIDE.

I WISH he would decide, mamma,
   I wish he would decide;
I've been a bridesmaid twenty times—
   When shall I be a bride?
My cousin Anne, my sister Fan,
   The nuptial-knot have tied;
Yet come what will, I'm single still—
   I wish he would decide.

He takes me to the play, mamma,
　　He brings me pretty books;
He woos me with his eyes, mamma,
　　Such speechless things he looks!
Where'er I roam—abroad, at home—
　　He lingers by my side;
Yet come what will, I'm single still—
　　I wish he would decide.

I throw out many hints, mamma,
　　I speak of other beaux,
I talk about domestic life,
　　And sing " They don't propose ";
But ah! how vain each piteous strain
　　His wavering heart to guide!
Do what I will, I'm single still—
　　I wish he would decide.

ANONYMOUS.

AN IDYL OF THE PERIOD.

I.

" COME right in—how are you, Fred ?
   Find a chair and have a light."
" Well, old boy, recovered yet
   From the Mathers' jam last night ? "
" Didn't dance ; the german 's old."
   " Didn't you ? . I had to lead—
Awful bore—but where where you ? "
   " Sat it out with Molly Meade ;
Jolly little girl she is—
   Said she didn't care to dance,
'D rather have a quiet chat ;
   Then she gave me such a glance !
Gave me her bouquet to hold,
   Asked me to draw off her glove ;
Then, of course, I squeezed her hand,
   Talked about my wasted life,
Said my sole salvation must
   Be a true and gentle wife.

Then, you know, I used my eyes ;
　She believed me, every word,
Almost said she loved me—Jove !
　Such a voice I never heard !—
Gave me some symbolic flower,
　Had a meaning, Oh, so sweet !
Don't know where it is, I'm sure,
　Must have dropped it in the street.
How I spooned ! and she—ha ! ha !
　Well, I know it wasn't right ;
But she did believe me so,
　That I—kissed her.　Pass a light."

II.

" Mollie Meade—well, I declare !
　Who'd have thought of seeing you,
After what occurred last night,
　Out here on the avenue ?
Oh, you awful, awful girl !
　There, don't blush—I saw it all."
" Saw all what ? "　" Ahem ! last night—
　At the Mathers' in the hall."

" Oh, you horrid ! where were you ?
  Wasn't he an awful goose ?
Most men must be caught ; but he
  Ran his neck right in the noose.
I was almost dead to dance ;
  I'd have done it if I could ;
But old Gray said I must stop,
  And I promised ma I would ;
So I looked up sweet and said
  I had rather talk with him—
Hope he didn't see my face ;
  Luckily the lights were dim.
Then, Oh, how he squeezed my hand !
  And he looked up in my face
With his great, big, lovely eyes—
  Really it's a dreadful case !
He was all in earnest, too ;
  But I really thought I'd have to laugh—
When he kissed a flower I gave,
  Looking, Oh, like such a calf !
I suppose he has it now
  In a wine-glass on his shelves ;

It's a mystery to me
   Why men will deceive themselves.
'Saw him kiss me!'   Oh, you wretch!
   Well, he begged so hard for one,
And I thought there'd no one know—
   So I let him, just for fun!
I know it wasn't really right
   To trifle with his feelings, dear;
But men are such conceited things,
   They need a lesson once a year."

ANONYMOUS.

A TINY TRAGEDY.

PERIOD—*Indefinite.*   SCENE—*Anywhere.*

ACT I.

A SHADY nook—
A rippling brook—
      Moonlight;
A garden chair—
A youthful pair—
      Delight!

ACT II.

Troth plighted oft
In accents soft.
       Oh, bliss!
Vow endless love—
(Cease, laughing Jove!)
       And kiss.

ACT III.

A jealous thought—
The mischief 's wrought.
       Untrue?
A haughty pout—
A cutting flout.
       Adieu!

ACT IV.

A vessel starts:
In distant parts
       He'll roam.

A hapless maid
By anguish swayed—
　　　　At home.

ACT V.

Years onward fleet:
Old lovers meet
　　　　And show,
As often found,
Doubts without ground.
　　　　Tableau!

ALF. CARNIE,

The Parchment-Paper Series.

Fair Words about Fair Woman,

Gathered from the Poets by O. B. BUNCE. With Nine Illustrations from Designs by WILL H. LOW. Crown 8vo. Cloth, extra gilt, price, $3.00.

This volume is a collection of poems in exaltation of woman. It is divided into Eight Evenings. The First Evening is devoted principally to poems addressed simply to the sex—splendid generalizations of the virtues and charms of women ; the Second Evening consists of selections from the old English poets ; the Third is devoted exclusively to Tennyson ; the Fourth is a selection from Irish and Scotch poets ; the Fifth includes excerpts from Greek, Italian, French, German, Spanish, and other foreign poets ; the Sixth consists of selections from modern English and American poets ; the Seventh is devoted to poems exalting woman at the fireside, as wife and mother ; and the Eighth and last to woman as the heroine of romance.

Fifty Perfect Poems.

A Collection of Fifty Acknowledged Masterpieces, by English and American Poets. Selected and Edited by CHARLES A. DANA and ROSSITER JOHNSON.

With Seventy-two Original Illustrations from Drawings by Alfred Fredericks, Frank Millet, Will Low, T. W. Dewing, W. T. Smedley, F. O. C. Darley, Swain Gifford, Harry Fenn, Appleton Brown, William Sartain, Arthur Quartley, J. D. Woodward, Walter Satterlee, S. G. McCutcheon, and J. E. Kelley. The engravings, which are very fine and artistic, are printed on Japanese silk paper, and mounted on the page, producing a unique and beautiful effect.

Large 8vo. Cloth, gilt extra, price, $9.00; also bound in silk, $10.00.

New York: D. APPLETON & CO., 1, 3, & 5 Bond Street.

A Thousand Flashes of French Wit, Wisdom, and Wickedness.

Collected and translated by J. DE FINOD.

A collection of wise and brilliant sayings from French writers, making a rich and piquant book of fresh quotations.

One volume, 16mo, cloth, price, $1.00.

New York: D. APPLETON & CO., 1, 3, & 5 Bond Street.

Uncle Remus:
His Songs and his Sayings.

THE FOLK-LORE OF THE OLD PLANTATION.

By JOEL CHANDLER HARRIS.

". . . Mr. Harris's book may be looked on in a double light—either as a pleasant volume recounting the stories told by a typical old colored man to a child, or as a valuable contribution to our somewhat meager folk-lore. . . . To Northern readers the story of Brer (Brother—Brudder) Rabbit may be novel. To those familiar with plantation life, who have listened to these quaint old stories, who have still tender reminiscences of some good old mauma who told these wondrous adventures to them when they were children, Brer Rabbit, the Tar Baby, and Brer Fox, come back again with all the past pleasures of younger days."—*New York Times.*

Well illustrated from Drawings by F. S. Church, whose humorous animal drawings are so well known, and J. H. Moser, of Georgia.

1 vol., 12mo, cloth.   Price, $1.50.

New York: D. APPLETON & CO., 1, 3, & 5 Bond Street.

www.ingramcontent.com/pod-product-compliance
Lightning Source LLC
Chambersburg PA
CBHW032200010726
47493CB00008BA/2762